HUCKLEBUG

written by: Stephen Cosgrove
illustrated by: Robin James

Published by Creative Education, Inc., 123 South Broad Street, Mankato, Minnesota 56001. Copyright ©1975 by Serendipity Communications, Ltd. Printed in the United States of America. All rights reserved.

Library of Congress Cataloging in Publication Data

Cosgrove, Stephen.
 Hucklebug.

 SUMMARY: Young Berry Hucklebug runs away from his village rather than help gather food, but soon regrets his decision.
 [1. Community life—Fiction]   I. James, Robin.   II. Title.
PZ7.C8187Hu 1978   [E]   78-11453
ISBN 0-87191-657-6

Dedicated to every tiny living thing.
S. Cosgrove

On a bright spring morning, in a small village of Hucklebugs, in someone's backyard, Berry Hucklebug was born. There was nothing different about Berry. He was ordinary and fun-loving.

For months and months after Berry was born, he played with the other bugs of the village. They would play hide-and-go-seek, and "hucks" and robbers.

Early one day Berry was called before the mayor of the little village. "Berry," he said, "you are of age now and you must work as the others of the village do. Food for all must be gathered by all."

"Me?" said an unbelieving Berry. "But I don't want to. I want to stay with my friends. I want to run and play in the sunshine."

Sternly, the mayor looked down at Berry and said, "Everyone must work in this village, and you are no exception. Please start tomorrow morning. That is all. You may go now."

Sadly, little Hucklebug walked back to his playmates. But since the mayor's news, he didn't feel like joining his friends. So Berry sat in a corner and pouted. "What am I going to do?" he said. "The mayor is picking on me because I'm small."

Suddenly an idea came to him. "I'll run away and live by myself. Nobody will bother me then." With that, Berry went straight to his room. He rummaged through his butterfly wings and old bumblebee tails until he found his yellow bandana. Carefully he laid it on the floor and began packing.

He packed his hand-knitted antenna warmers for cold winter mornings. He packed his favorite red T-shirt with the big bold gold "B." And last but not least, he packed his new orange sneakers for special occasions. Then Berry tied his bandana into a big careful knot, threw it over his shoulder and slipped away from the village.

The farther he went, the happier Berry became. There were beautiful flowers all around him. He saw forests of silver-blue grass, and a blue sky overhead. "What do I need of that old Hucklebug Village?" he laughed brightly. "Out here I have everything I need." And, snickering, he added: "There's no one to tell me what to do."

Once or twice he came upon some of his fellow bugs gathering food for the village. As soon as he saw them, he would quickly jump behind a tall weed. From there he laughed and sneered at them, for they had not thought to run away.

After a time, Berry came to a rise in the path. Creeping slowly to the top, he discovered a furry caterpillar crawling along. Down below him he saw a giant's house. "WOW!" exclaimed Berry. "I bet it would be a lot of fun to go down there!"

Just then the caterpillar turned and frowned at the runaway. "If you're thinking of going down there," he grumbled, "I'd think again."

Laughingly, Berry twisted the caterpillar's antennae together. Then he raced down the hill to the huge house below. "That dumb caterpillar didn't know what he was talking about," he said. "Nobody can tell me what to do!"

He ran, jumped and giggled onto the lawn, and there he found the most amazing toys that he'd ever seen in his entire life. There were gigantic squirt guns, and mammoth baseball gloves which were large enough to live in if he wanted. He saw a beach ball that was at least 100 miles high. Berry felt as though he had found Hucklebug heaven.

Berry climbed to the top of the beach ball and began bouncing up and down. He was doing flips and jumping so high he didn't notice that the door of the house was open. Some giant kids were coming out to play.

The beach ball went flying! Berry went flying! The kids were playing kickball. Berry picked himself up from the cool grass. "What was that?" he asked. Slowly he turned, and for the first time, saw the giants. "WOW! They are big, but maybe I can play anyway."

With that he ran over to join in their fun, but the giants didn't see him. Berry dodged from side to side. He managed to avoid being squashed by shoes as big as his house in the Hucklebug village.

"Hey kids," he shouted, "can I play too?" The giants were so busy laughing and giggling that they didn't hear him.

Just by chance, one of the giant boys spied Berry standing in the grass. Carefully he leaned down and looked Berry right in the eye. "What a funny-looking bug," he said. Then he called to his friends to come and look at Berry.

Now let me tell you, Berry was a little scared. In fact, he was a lot scared. He wanted to run away, but the giants blocked his path.

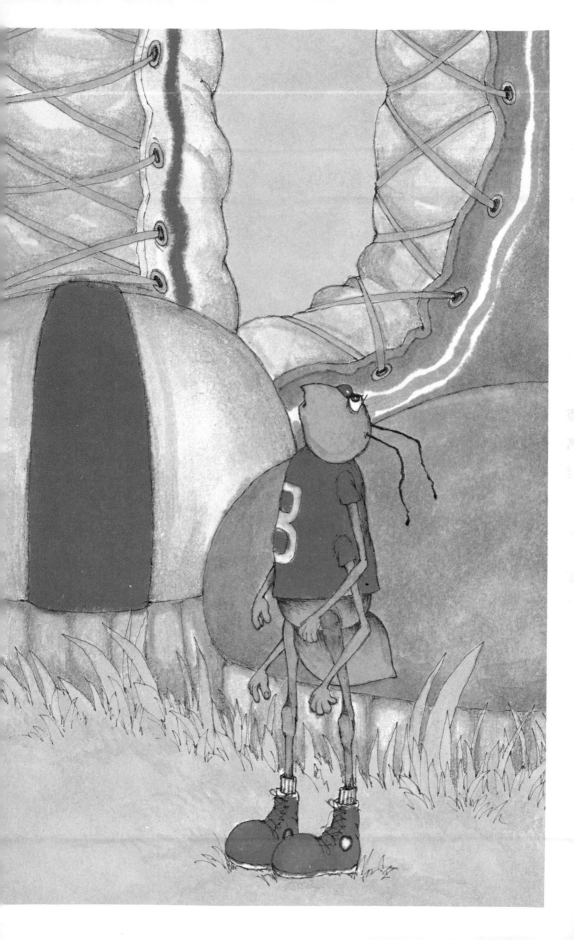

With a mischievous grin, one of the giant boys pointed his squirt gun at Berry. Berry caught a full blast of water in his fuzzy face.

He was really scared now, and started to run away. Every place he turned there was a giant trying either to step on him or to catch him. Scrambling over a leaf and under a twig, Berry tearfully made his escape up the path.

Puffing and panting, he found his way back up to the top of the hill. The old caterpillar was still trying to untie his antennae, so Berry untied them for him.

"You were right, Mr. Caterpillar," said Berry. "I shouldn't have gone down there. I'm confused, and I don't know what to do. It was a mistake to run away from home. Now I am ashamed to go back." Berry leaned against a toadstool and began to cry large, purple Hucklebug tears.

The wise old caterpillar smiled a little smile and said, "Little Hucklebug, if you have learned from your mistake, it is not a mistake, but a lesson. As you grow older you will make other mistakes, but never be afraid to admit them. Go home now and do what needs to be done. Always remember the lesson you've learned today."

Berry wiped a tear from his eye. Then, thanking the caterpillar for his kindness, he headed home to the Hucklebug village.

He walked through the beautiful flowers and the forests of silver-blue grass. Entering the village, he bravely marched up to the mayor and said, "Mr. Mayor, I'm really sorry for running away. I've learned from my mistake, and it is a lesson I will always remember. I promise that I'll never run away again."

The mayor patted Berry on the head and told him that he was forgiven. Since he had run away, though, he would have to work an extra day as punishment. Then the kind mayor smiled and told Berry to play for the rest of the day.

Berry Hucklebug gleefully skipped away to join his friends . . . at home.

Mistakes are always mistakes,
Or so I've heard them say . . .
But if it teaches a lesson,
The mistake will go away.